W9-CPE-837

Frances Frog's Forever Friend

by Barbara deRubertis • illustrated by R.W. Alley

THE KANE PRESS / NEW YORK

Alpha Betty's Class

Alexander Anteater

Bobby Baboon

Corky Cub

Dilly Dog

Hanna Hippo

Eddie Elephant

STAR of the BOOK

Frances Frog

Gertie Gorilla

Lana Llama

Izzy Impala

Jeremy Jackrabbit

Kylie Kangaroo

Maxwell Moose

Nina Nandu

Oliver Otter

Polly Porcupine

Quentin Quokka

Rosie Raccoon

Sammy Skunk

Tessa Tiger

Umma Ungka

Victor Vicuna

Walter Warthog

Xavier Ox

Yoko Yak

Zachary Zebra

Alpha Betty

Library of Congress Cataloging-in-Publication Data

deRubertis, Barbara.
Frances Frog's forever friend / by Barbara deRubertis ; Illustrated by R.W. Alley.
p. cm. — (Animal antics A to Z)
Summary: Frances Frog and Felicity Fox are best friends, but sometimes
Frances's foolishness is no fun for Felicity.
ISBN 978-1-57565-317-4 (library binding : alk. paper) — ISBN 978-1-57565-310-5 (pbk. : alk. paper)
[1. Best friends—Fiction. 2. Friendship—Fiction. 3. Behavior—Fiction. 4. Frogs—Fiction. 5. Foxes—
Fiction. 6. Alphabet. 7. Humorous stories.] I. Alley, R. W. (Robert W.), ill. II. Title.
PZ7.D4475Fr 2010
[E]—dc22   2009049879

1 3 5 7 9 10 8 6 4 2

First published in the United States of America in 2010 by Kane Press, Inc.
Printed in the United States of America
WOZ0710

Series Editor: Juliana Hanford
Book Design: Edward Miller

Animal Antics A to Z is a registered trademark of Kane Press, Inc.

www.kanepress.com

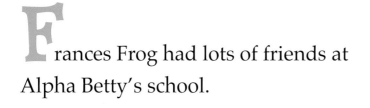

Frances Frog had lots of friends at Alpha Betty's school.

But her favorite friend did not go to her school. Her friend's name was Felicity Fox.

Frances and Felicity were very different.
Frances was bumpy.
Felicity was furry.

Frances was fancy.
Felicity was plain.

Frances was frisky.
Felicity was quiet.

Frances was funny and often laughed.
Felicity was serious and sometimes frowned.

And Frances was frequently a
little foolish.
But Felicity was never, ever foolish.
Still, each was the other's favorite friend.

Felicity had fun with Frances.

Frances helped Felicity feel brave,
even when she was afraid.

Frances could always count on Felicity.

If Frances had a problem, Felicity
could often fix it.

One fine day, Frances and Felicity
planned a picnic.

Each packed her own favorite foods.

Frances Frog had French fries, deep-fried fritters, and fizzy pop.

Felicity Fox had fresh fruit, fish tacos, and frozen yogurt.

"What a fantastic, fried-food feast!" said Frances.

"What fine, flavorful, low-fat food!" said Felicity.

In five minutes, Frances had finished
ALL of her food.

A few minutes later, she felt awful.

"I am too full. My tummy is stuffed.
In fact," said Frances, "I feel SICK!"

"Oh, Frances!" Felicity frowned.
"You stuffed yourself with fatty foods.
AND you ate too fast.
That was very foolish!"

But Felicity felt sorry for Frances.

So she helped her floppy friend
shuffle home.

One fall afternoon, Frances and
Felicity played football.

Frances kicked the football far
down the field.

Felicity made a fantastic catch.

She ran up the field very fast.

Frances flipped her feet. She flapped her
arms. And she fluttered her fingers.

Poor Felicity was flustered and confused!
She stumbled and fumbled the ball.

Frances flopped on top of it.

Felicity folded her arms.

"Sometimes you don't play fair, Frances.

That was a foolish thing to do.

And I wish you would apologize!"

"Oh, Felicity!" Frances laughed.
"I was just having fun!"

Felicity frowned. "It wasn't fun for ME."

One sunny afternoon, Frances and
Felicity went to the swimming pool.

"I am not a good swimmer, Frances,"
said Felicity.
"So I will lie on my fish float."

Carefully, Felicity stretched out on her float.

Then she gave Frances a reminder.
"No. More. Foolishness," she said.
"Promise?"

"Fine," laughed Frances.

Frances flew off the diving board.

She did a fancy flip.

Then she fell on the water with a foamy *ker-FLUP!*

She flapped her arms and flopped her feet.

Water flooded over Felicity.

And she was flipped right off her fish float!

Felicity was frantic.
And she was AFRAID!

"Help! Help!" cried Felicity.

Frances flew into action.

She flipped Felicity back onto
her fish float.

Huffing and puffing, Frances
pulled Felicity to safety.

Felicity fussed and fumed as Frances lifted
her out of the water.

Felicity was furious.
"That was NOT funny, Frances," said Felicity.
"That was a VERY foolish thing to do!"

Frances felt AWFUL.

"I'm so sorry, Felicity," said Frances.
"I did not mean to frighten you.
You are my forever friend!"

For the first time, Frances looked REALLY sorry.

"I forgive you," said Felicity.
"Sometimes you are a foolish frog.
But you are a fast helper!"

Finally, instead of frowning, Felicity smiled.
"Frances, you are my forever friend, too."

From then on, Frances Frog was a much kinder and more careful friend.

She still liked having fun.

But she always made sure Felicity Fox was having fun, too!

FUN FACTS

- **Home:** Everywhere in the world except Antarctica!
- **Baby frogs:** Most frogs begin life in the water as tadpoles. After losing their tails and growing legs, they can also live on land.
- **Size:** Some frogs are so tiny they can sit on your fingertip. Some can grow to be over a foot long, not including their legs!
- **Favorite foods:** Mostly insects or worms, but some frogs also eat small rodents, snakes, and other frogs!
- **Did You Know?** Long, strong legs make frogs excellent leapers. And webbed feet make them speedy swimmers!

LOOK BACK

Learning to identify letter sounds (phonemes) at the beginning, middle, and end of words is called "phonemic awareness."

- The word *fun* <u>begins</u> with the *f* sound. Listen to the words on page 7 being read again. When you hear a word that <u>begins</u> with the *f* sound, take a tiny hop forward and say the word!

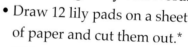

- **Challenge:** Listen to the words in the word bank below being read aloud. When a word <u>begins</u> with the *f* sound, hop forward. When a word <u>ends</u> with the *f* sound, hop backward.

frog	puff	fox	cuff	fun	cliff	four	half
	fur	calf	huff	fish	stuff	fast	fix

TRY THIS!

Frances Frog's Lily Pad Words

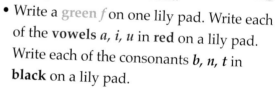

- Draw 12 lily pads on a sheet of paper and cut them out.*
- Write a green *f* on one lily pad. Write each of the **vowels** *a, i, u* in **red** on a lily pad. Write each of the consonants *b, n, t* in **black** on a lily pad.
- Make as many words as you can with the green *f* at the <u>beginning</u>, a **red vowel** in the <u>middle</u>, and a **black consonant** at the <u>end</u>.

*A printable, ready-to-use activity page with 12 lily pads is available at: www.kanepress.com/AnimalAntics/FrancesFrog.html

(Words you can make: fan, fat, fib, fin, fit, fun)

FOR MORE ACTIVITIES, go to Frances Frog's website: www.kanepress.com/AnimalAntics/FrancesFrog.html
You'll also find a recipe for Frances Frog's Fresh Fruit Salad!